INVISIBLE ENEMIES

A Handbook on Pandemics That Have Shaped Our World

Hwee Goh

Illustrated by **David Liew**

 **Marshall Cavendish**
Children

Reprinted 2020

Published by Marshall Cavendish Children
An imprint of Marshall Cavendish International

A member of the
Times Publishing Group

Other Marshall Cavendish Offices:
Marshall Cavendish Corporation, 800 Westchester Ave, Suite N-641, Rye
Brook, NY 10573, USA • Marshall Cavendish International (Thailand) Co Ltd,
253 Asoke, 16th Flr, Sukhumvit 21 Road, Klongtoey Nua, Wattana, Bangkok
10110, Thailand • Marshall Cavendish (Malaysia) Sdn Bhd, Times Subang,
Lot 46, Subang Hi-Tech Industrial Park, Batu Tiga, 40000 Shah Alam,
Selangor Darul Ehsan, Malaysia

National Library Board, Singapore Cataloguing-in-Publication Data

Name(s): Goh, Hwee. | Liew, David, illustrator.
Title: Invisible enemies : a handbook on pandemics that have shaped our
world / Hwee Goh ; illustrated by David Liew.
Description: Singapore : Marshall Cavendish Children, [2020]
Identifier(s): OCN 1148958747 | ISBN 978-981-48-9345-9 (hardback)
Subject(s): LCSH: Epidemics--Juvenile literature. | Communicable diseases
--Juvenile literature.
Classification: DDC 614.4--dc23

Printed in Singapore

CONTENTS

THE ENEMY IS INVISIBLE

There is a Chinese saying, 暗箭难防 (àn jìan nán fáng). It means that when an enemy is invisible, it is hard to prevent arrows coming at your back. Here's the **game changer**: if the enemy is something you can't see, but something you can learn all about, that's when you can fight back!

Battlefield BODY

Battlefields are not just where soldiers fight, but battles are also fought against disease. Tiny invaders called germs, which are usually viruses or bacteria, can attack our bodies.

It's **INSIDE** you!

Did You Know?

When infections spread through a community or city of people, it becomes an **epidemic**. On a larger scale, when the epidemic crosses countries and becomes global, it is called a **pandemic**.

SQUISH!

Gods' Vengeance

In ancient myth and superstition, disease was often thought to be a punishment from the gods. However, Hippocrates (460–375 BC), known as the father of medicine, believed that disease came from man and his environment.

Hippocratic Oath

In many countries, newly-trained doctors still say the Hippocratic oath. This is a pledge that they make to treat patients to the best of their ability. Although known as the Hippocratic oath, we cannot be sure it was written by Hippocrates himself. The oath dates back to ancient Greece, when the roots of modern medicine began.

It's Just Bad Air

Before the mid 1800s, people used to believe in **miasma** (mee-az-mur), that disease was caused by bad air and foul smells. This is how **malaria** was named — in Italian, "mala" means "bad" and "aria" means "air". Malaria is one of the first diseases to be discovered. It is actually caused by a parasite spread through mosquitoes. It is now curable by quinine, made from the bark of a tree.

The Theory of Germs

French microbiologist Louis Pasteur debunked the "bad air" theory through many experiments. If he boiled milk, killed the bacteria within, and sealed it, the milk did not go sour. In other words, it is the bacteria in the air that causes food to spoil.

Did You Know?

Have you noticed that some milk or juice cartons you see in the supermarket don't need to go in the fridge? Such long life or UHT (Ultra Heat Treated) food and drinks are preserved by pasteurisation. Germs are killed, before the food is sealed, to keep it from going bad.

Early Experiments

In 1914, a German microbiologist got his assistant who had a cold, to blow his nose. He mixed the assistant's mucus into a salt solution, filtered it and put it into the noses of 12 colleagues. Four of them came down with the cold. He tried this again on 36 students — 15 of them fell sick.

Did You Know?

Over time, scientists began to understand that disease was caused by **minute** organisms invading the body, and could be passed between people.

What's That?

minute (mai-newt): Very tiny.

Otto,
I like Dr Kruse but next semester I DON'T want to take his class OK?

Dr Kruse's Class 1915

Making Air Without Air

Long ago, people knew that leaving grapes and grain in a container for a long time produced wine or beer. But they did not know how and why. Louis Pasteur confirmed that the microorganism, yeast, is responsible for turning sugar from the grain or grapes into alcohol and carbon dioxide.

Stomping Grapes!

The practice of stomping on grapes to make wine is said to be almost 6,000 years old. It is now illegal in some countries for wine makers to do this although others offer it as a tourist attraction. However, there is one theory that this is how yeast, a type of fungus, gets into the grape mixture. It is transferred from the feet! Hic!

I just LOVE Madame Raisin's PURPLE SOCKS!

Those aren't socks, Gaston...

The Enemy of My Enemy is My Friend

During World War I, French scientist Félix d'Hérelle was called in to study a severe spread of dysentery among soldiers. He filtered the soldiers' stool for shigella, the bacteria that causes diarrhoea. On the **Petri dish**, he discovered a micro battlefield — the shigella had been infected by a virus (also from the soldiers' bodies) which was killing them off!

What's That?
A **Petri dish** is a shallow glass dish with a thin glass cover. In 1877, German doctor Julius Richard <u>Petri</u> created this lab staple that is used to this day.

Er... could you hurry up a little bit? Dr d'Hérelle needs more samples...

Bacteria Killers

These bacteria-killing viruses are called **phage**. They live alongside the bacteria they conquer. Félix d'Hérelle found that the more phage there was in the infected person's body, the sooner the person recovered.

Did You Know?
Phage (fay-j) is no longer used to cure the sick because of the need to use a 'live' virus. However, studies are being done to see if it might work against bacteria that are hard to kill and resistant to drugs.

Milkmaids and the World's First Vaccine

In 1796, country doctor Edward Jenner performed the world's first vaccination. He wondered why the milkmaids who contracted cowpox were immune to the much more deadly **smallpox**. So he collected the pus from a cowpox blister of a milkmaid and transferred it to an eight-year-old boy. Six weeks later, he infected the boy with smallpox and the boy did not fall ill.

Did You Know?
Smallpox was completely eliminated in 1979. Before that, it was dubbed the worst killer ever, wiping out up to half a billion people in the 20th century.

Great effort, Marcel...
But I think you haven't understood fully...
For our vaccines, the MAD DOGS we need are
MAD as in that they are crazy with RABIES
and not MAD as in that you got them
a bit MIFFED!

It's ALIVE!!!

Based on this principle of using a weaker version of a virus to 'teach' a human body to become immune to the actual, more deadly virus, Louis Pasteur developed the rabies vaccine. To this day, weakened versions of a virus or harmful bacteria are used to vaccinate children against diseases like measles and polio.

Mouldy Medicine

It was said that the Egyptians used to apply a paste made from mouldy bread to treat infected wounds. But it wasn't until 1928 that Englishman Alexander Fleming left his bacteria research out. When he checked his Petri dishes, he found that the harmful bacteria Staphylococcus steered clear of an area where some mould had grown. This mould became the common **antibiotic**, penicillin!

Doctor Ankibak...
The bread has to be
MOULDY...
Not FRESH and HOT!

But it was an
EMERGENCY!

What's That?

Antibiotics are a group of medicines used to fight bacterial infections.

I Can See Clearly Now

Early microscopes used a lens and light to magnify the view by up to a thousand times, but this was not enough to see viruses. In the 1930s, the **electron microscope** was developed. It uses high voltage to charge electrons within a vacuum, to produce images up to a few million times bigger.

Did You Know?
The **electron microscope** was another game changer for the study of viruses. It allowed scientists to study the structure of viruses and learn how to fight them.

PATIENT ZERO

It is 20 February 2003. Singapore's **Patient Zero** stays in a hotel in Hong Kong, where a few doors away, a doctor from Guangdong, China, is battling an unknown fever. It is likely that Patient Zero touches a contaminated surface, possibly a lift button, that the sick doctor had touched before.

Did You Know?
Patient zero is commonly used to refer to the first patient to bring an infectious disease into a community. In medical science, the term is **"index case"**. In California, US in the 1980s, a man believed to be the first ever patient with AIDS was labelled "patient O" (meaning that he was from "<u>o</u>utside" the state of California). This was wrongly read as patient zero.

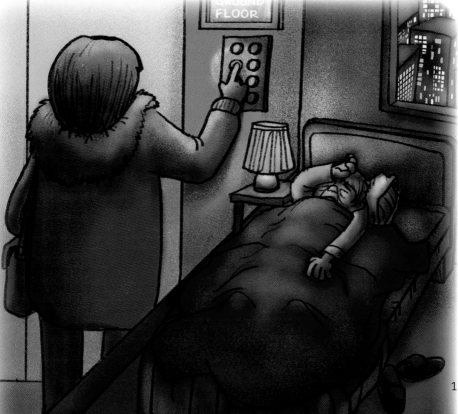

13

Mystery Illness Arrives in Singapore

Back in Singapore, Patient Zero develops a cough. When the 23-year-old goes with her mum to visit her paternal grandmother at Tan Tock Seng Hospital, her mum sends her to see a doctor there. Her fever is a mild 37.6°C (99.7°F). But her chest X-ray gives the doctor a shock.

Did You Know?
On an X-ray, pneumonia or lung infection appears as white cloudy patches on the lungs.

Shock Waves

Meanwhile, people who have visited or treated Patient Zero start to fall ill. At the same time, there is a report from Guangdong, China of an **atypical** pneumonia that has caused some deaths. In early March, more reports of this mystery disease emerge worldwide.

What's That?
atypical: Not typical.

Did You Know?
In general, when the body battles with an invading virus, this is when the patient has a fever.

Invasion by Virus

The virus infects by invading a healthy 'host' cell, tricks it into shutting down and turns it into a 'virus factory', making lots of copies of itself. When the virus army is built, copied viruses spill out and repeat this process while the original host cell is destroyed. For SARS, this often happens in the lungs.

VIRUS IN DISGUISE

HEALTHY CELLS

ATYPICAL PNEUMONIA   RAPID SPREAD   DEATHS   REGULAR TREATMENT NOT WORKING   SARS

INDEX CASE

What is SARS?

On 15 March 2003, this mystery illness that does not respond to standard treatment, gets an official name: Severe Acute Respiratory Syndrome (SARS). It takes a few more weeks for doctors to map out what it is, how long it **incubates** and when it spreads.

What's That?

An **incubation period** refers to the time when a person is first infected to when he/she starts to show symptoms (signs) of illness.

War Zone

Singapore's Tan Tock Seng Hospital prepares to battle this new disease that's proving to be highly contagious. Patient Zero is put in isolation, where the air in the room is not circulated out. The hospital's A & E (Accident and Emergency) Department sets up a 'fever tent' to see patients and sort them according to their risk for SARS.

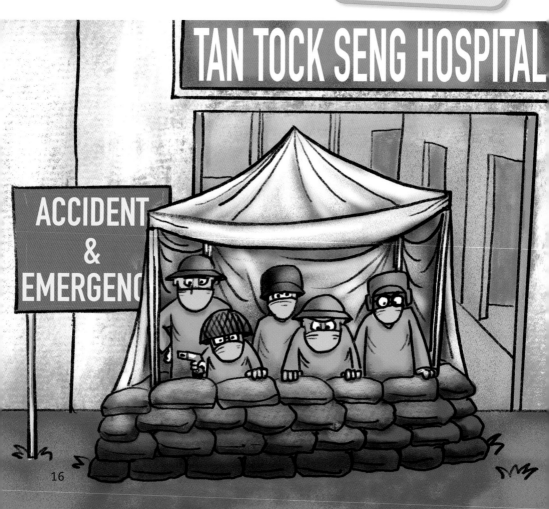

Atchoo! Cough, Cough!

When a sick person talks, coughs or sneezes, he releases droplets loaded with the virus into the air around him. This could get passed to another person who inhales it, or touches a droplet and then touches his own mouth, nose or eyes.

Ice Cream Fund

Doctors, nurses and hospital attendants are the most vulnerable due to their constant exposure to the virus. It is vital that they observe strict rules against contamination with their PPE.

The staff start an Ice Cream Fund to fine fellow workers who lapse on these measures. It is S$5 each time. Once there is S$30 in the fund, a round of ice cream is bought! The healthcare workers get so good at observing these rules, there isn't much money for ice cream in the end.

Singapore War Machine

The **outbreak** is a true test for Singapore. All healthcare workers have to take their temperatures daily to keep track of their health. 'Wide net' operations start with massive white boards **tracking** the movement of every patient who has been tested positive for SARS, to contain its spread.

What's That?

An **outbreak** of a disease happens when there is a new contagion, or when there are more cases than expected in a community.

Did You Know?

Contact tracing is a tedious and meticulous job of mapping a confirmed patient's movements and getting in touch with people he/she had been in close contact with. This is done within 24 hours.

Home Under the Law

Those who have been in contact with SARS patients are served Home Quarantine Orders, and are required under the law to stay home for 10 days. Discharged SARS patients have to stay home for two weeks. The aim is to stop transmission completely.

Are You HOT?

Doctors and scientists soon figure out that in the
case of SARS, an infected person very often has
a telltale fever. Temperature-taking becomes key.
Studies later find that if patients are isolated
before Day Five of their illness, they rarely pass it on.

SUPER SPREADERS

HONG KONG

The experience of Singapore's Patient Zero is for her, the greatest nightmare ever imagined. That one fateful stay in the Hong Kong hotel sees her bring back SARS to the first cluster of 109 patients. On 25 March 2003, her father is the first in Singapore to die of SARS, followed by her pastor, mother and uncle. As she recovers, new infection clusters spread throughout Singapore.

SINGAPORE

Did You Know?
There were two other Singaporean women staying in the same hotel as Patient Zero. One was her friend and the other was a tour guide. Both the women fall ill back in Singapore, get treated, and do not pass SARS on to others.

A League of Their Own

In Singapore, only five super spreaders account for more than half the number of total infections in the country.

- Super Spreader 1: Patient Zero
- Super Spreader 2: Nurse who attended to (1)
- Super Spreader 3: Patient in same hospital ward as (2)
- Super Spreader 4: Patient in same hospital ward as (1)
- Super Spreader 5: Brother of (4)

Typhoid Mary

The most famous patient zero is Irishwoman Mary Mallon, who moved to New York, US, and worked as a live-in cook. In 1907, investigators found that all the families Mary worked for developed typhoid fever, but Mary herself showed no symptoms. Believed to be responsible for the outbreak, Mary was arrested. This was before typhoid could be treated, and killed 10% of all who fell ill with it.

Did You Know?

Super spreaders cannot be identified in the beginning. Hence, the best strategy for preventing infection is still the same: isolate or separate the infected, and observe good hygiene habits.

Airborne Aerosols

It has been found that for every 10 people down with an infectious disease, only two are super spreaders. Scientists have not pinned down why, but there are a few possible reasons:

- The patient is very good at fighting the virus, so he/she doesn't fall very ill, but carries the disease and can pass it on.

- The patient is not so good at fighting the virus, so he/she has a heavy 'viral load' in the system.

- It is possible that high 'viral load' + wet cough is the worst combination — the wet cough becomes an 'aerosol spray', spewing the virus outward.

Some Like It Not

To test the concept of 'viral load', scientists in Singapore put the blood cells of their colleagues onto Petri dishes and infect the healthy cells with the SARS virus. On some blood samples, the SARS virus multiplies many times. On others, there is a much lower load of the virus.

Hong Kong's Index Case

SARS is documented to have first appeared in Guangdong, China. In early 2003, the first super spreader there, a fish seller, infects 30 doctors and nurses. One doctor flies to Hong Kong to attend a wedding and stays at the same hotel as Singapore's Patient Zero. This doctor infects more than 20 hotel guests, who go on their journeys and infect new clusters in Hanoi, Vietnam and Toronto, Canada.

Up the Pipes and All Fall Down

In late March 2003, more than 300 residents in a huge Kowloon, Hong Kong apartment complex fall ill at the same time, with 42 deaths. The origin of the SARS virus is traced to a man who had visited his brother there. As it turns out, the virus had spread through the sewage pipes, and possibly via droplets in the air.

Hell in Hanoi

From the Hong Kong hotel, a Chinese-American man travels to Hanoi, Vietnam, already ill by the time he arrives. He heads straight to a hospital and dies two weeks later, but not before infecting 38 healthcare workers including Infectious Diseases Specialist, Dr Carlo Urbani, from the **World Health Organization (WHO)**.

What's That?

The **World Health Organization (WHO)** focuses on health issues around the world, including preparing for, and responding to pandemics.

The First SARS Hero

DR CARLO URBANI
1956 ~ 2003

Dr WHO

Dr Carlo Urbani is widely credited as the first doctor to identify SARS and for saving many lives with his early detection of it. As he treats his patient, Dr Urbani receives reports of similar mystery illnesses across the world. The good doctor works hard to find out all he can about the virus and sends alerts to health authorities globally. Sadly, he dies of SARS within a month of being infected.

SARS Breaks Out

Singapore's Super Spreader 4 shared a ward with Patient Zero before she was isolated. This patient, discharged for his stomach ailment, goes to a different hospital a few days later, still unwell.

Did You Know?

When healthcare workers or visitors to a hospital fall sick, they see a doctor in another hospital — leading to a chain of new infections. A leading health official labels this hospital-to-hospital transmission the greatest **amplifier** of SARS.

Mixed Signals

Super Spreader 4 has a low grade fever, but his lungs are clear on an X-ray. He also has multiple illnesses that might cause a fever. It is a whole week before doctors catch on that he might have been infected with SARS in the previous hospital. By then, he has directly infected 62 people in a wave involving Singapore's public hospitals.

What's That?

amplifier: Something which makes the original much bigger.

SINGAPORE CAN, LAH!

SARS in Singapore is very much a war on the minds of the people. When the mystery illness strikes and the first deaths are reported in late March 2003, many fear this invisible enemy. The strategy, in response, is two-**pronged**:

(1) **Mind**: To empower the people not to fear, but to rally and fight this enemy together.

(2) **Medicine**: To find out, scientifically, as much as possible, about how this enemy behaves, to contain it.

We're in this together

What's That?

prong: Usually the ends of a fork. It also refers to separate parts of a plan or strategy.

It's All in the Mind

The Singapore government is aware that having the people's confidence, is half the battle won. It engages the people on national TV with regular updates. On the ground, there are many activities to fire up support for patients and healthcare workers. Millions of dollars are set aside to help companies affected by SARS.

Did You Know?

A Singapore PR (Permanent Resident) shows the world that life goes on very well indeed in spite of SARS. For a few months that year, he runs a campaign called "Singapore Can Lah" and live streams footage of bustling locations all around Singapore.

SARS = Singaporeans Are Really Scared

Making a dig at the naysayers for saying this is what SARS stands for, Singapore's leaders very gamely drink Sarsi, a sarsaparilla fizzy drink on national TV. In the Chinese dialect, Hokkien, "sar-si" sounds like "kill SARS"!

Weapons of Knowledge

Temperature-taking becomes an everyday event in schools because fever is the most obvious sign of SARS. Since SARS is passed by close contact, more than 700 people are issued Home Quarantine Orders to break any possible new transmissions. Under the law, these people risk going to jail if they leave home before their 10 days are up.

STRAWS WERE STILL COMMONLY USED THEN

USEFUL

NOT USEFUL

OVEN THERMOMETER

JOIN THE FIGHT AGAINST SARS

A Call to Arms

Scientists in Singapore get into battle mode. A **forensic pathologist** extracts samples of this yet-unknown virus from the dead, and the **genomics** team works on sequencing the **DNA** code of the virus. Another team develops a test kit which eventually gets commercially produced and sold.

What's That?

forensic pathology: The science of determining the cause of death by examining the dead body.

genomics: The science of the genetic material of cells.

DNA: Deoxyribonucleic acid. This is the genetic or hereditary material in humans and almost all organisms. It has a double strand gene sequence.

Did You Know?

Scientists worldwide also rush to sequence the DNA of SARS. On 12 April 2003, the team in Vancouver, Canada does it first! Like most such viruses, there is still no cure for SARS, but work continues on developing a SARS vaccine.

Codebreaking Continues

The Singapore team ploughs on. By now, they know that SARS is an **RNA** virus that **mutates** very slightly. Within a week, they produce five different strains from the different infection clusters within Singapore. This becomes a genetic map together with the strains from Canada, Hong Kong and Vietnam.

What's That?

RNA: Ribonucleic acid. This is a single strand gene sequence and it is unstable.

mutation: A change in gene structure. If a virus mutates fast, it'll be hard to develop a test kit or vaccine for it. Fortunately, the SARS RNA was mostly stable and changed very little.

Out of the Blue

Singapore is declared SARS-free by end May 2003. Very strangely, one SARS case pops up in September in a 27-year-old lab researcher. Tests show that he was infected by the same strain as one of the earliest SARS patients. This also happened in other labs in China and Taiwan, highlighting the necessary but real risks of working with live viruses.

Epic Epidemiology

Epidemiology, which has the same root word as "epidemic" is derived from the Greek word for "epi", meaning "upon" and "demos", meaning "people". For infectious diseases that fall upon a community, epidemiology is the backbone of any battle plan. Data is collected on the who, what, when, where and why/how of each case.

Did You Know?

When SARS broke out in 2003, the WHO relied on massive amounts of information gathered from all the SARS-affected countries, in an effort to share early observations, so more deaths could be prevented.

EPIDEMIC
It's ON YOU OK?

HIPPOCRATES IS STILL IN THIS BOOK?

HE OFFERED THE WRITERS A PACKAGE DEAL!

The Grand Round

The grand round is traditionally done in hospitals every morning, when doctors gather in the ward to discuss patients and their cases. In 2003, even before the mystery illness is identified, the WHO in Geneva holds **virtual** grand rounds with doctors all over the world.

Winning by Numbers

For an unknown disease like SARS, early epidemiology is extremely important for scientists to derive patterns of infection, such as:

- Total number of infections, and of these, how many die (**case fatality rate**).
- Who were infected (healthcare workers and relatives of patients are at greater risk).
- How they were likely infected (person-to-person contact).
- The age of those infected (children were not as affected as the elderly).

Pandemic Prevented

Besides Singapore, 30 other countries also report SARS cases. The number is more than 8,000 and there are about 900 deaths. The WHO considers it an epidemic and credits close cooperation among countries for preventing it from reaching a global, pandemic level.

Did You Know?

In Singapore, the quick resolution to SARS and the lessons learnt point to this experience as a rehearsal for the Next Big One, a new invisible enemy that is bound to strike again.

Disease X

The WHO has a ranking of killer diseases so that priority can be put into research and prevention. Under this list of known diseases, there is a "Disease X". This recognises the next unknown enemy that might appear any time, and the need to do everything possible to prepare for it.

IGNORANCE IS (NOT) BLISS

Whatcha lookin' at?

Before the 16th century, there is no running water and no sewage systems. Rats are a common sight on the stinky streets. On top of this, there is no knowledge of germs and how they spread. When outbreaks happen, fighting the disease is akin to flying blind in battle.

But we're MICE!

Shhh... we're mice ACTORS We're PLAYING rats for this panel!

A Peek at the Plague

There are three recorded great pandemics of plague. It is only much later that scientists discover that the bacterium, *Yersinia pestis*, is the micro-monster responsible. Fleas bite infected rats and other animals, and go on to bite humans, infecting them with the **bubonic plague**.

It's not too late to call the PIED PIPER is it?

Did You Know?
Bubonic plague causes buboes, very swollen and painful lymph nodes under the arms, and at the neck and groin. If untreated, this could lead to infection in the blood, and death.

Death Doctors

Plague doctors in the 1600s believe that miasma, or bad air, is the cause of the illness. They put on a beak-like mask filled with herbs to ward off the toxic smells, wear glass goggles and carry a cane to avoid directly touching patients.

POMANDER

Did You Know?

Pneumonic plague happens when *Yersinia pestis* infects the lungs. It is less common but more deadly than the bubonic plague, and could spread from human to human.

Teeth Tell Tales

The Justinian Plague is the first recorded plague pandemic in history. It took place in the 6th century and killed 30–50 million people, or about half the world's population then. Scientists are able to confirm this, through traces of *Yersinia pestis* found in the teeth of skeletons dug up from that era.

TOOTH FAIRY CSI

The Black Death

The Black Death (1346–1353) wiped out millions and is believed to have killed up to a third of the people in Europe at that time. There are various theories as to why it was called **black**:

- The plague was said to have reached Europe in ships from the **Black** Sea, which were full of dead sailors with **black** boils on their bodies.

- The common **black** rat was in early theories, believed to be the cause of the illness (not the fleas on them).

Corpse Catapults

Bioterrorism is not a modern weapon. In a 14th century Latin account, an invading Mongol army attacks the Italian city of Caffa (now in Ukraine) by catapulting corpses into the city. These are bodies of Mongol soldiers, dead from the plague, which soon infect the townspeople. As the people flee, they bring the disease further west into Europe. (At that time, the Mongols thought it was the stench of the dead bodies that killed!)

What's That?

bioterrorism: A deliberate attack by releasing bacteria, viruses or other germs that cause illness or death.

Did You Know?

The US Centres for Disease Control and Prevention (CDC) lists the bubonic plague as a "Category A bioterrorism agent", which reflects the possibility that it could still be used as a military weapon.

LDEN HORDE
RECYCLING
CENTRE

If dying from the plague wasn't bad enough...

Extraordinary Eyam

In September 1665, a flea-infested bundle of blankets makes its way to a tailor's shop. In a week, the tailor's assistant is dead. The Black Death has arrived in the English village of Eyam. Knowing that if they left town, they might spread the **plague** further, Eyam residents decide to sacrifice themselves. For 14 months, nobody goes in and out of Eyam. Food is left at the edge of town, and coins placed in return. At the end of this, 260 out of about 800 Eyam residents die, but the plague does not spread.

Did You Know?

For 300 years after, the Black Death continues to **plague** the rest of Europe, causing spots of epidemics until the last one in London in 1665.

What's That?

plague: Also used as a verb to mean continually troubled by something.

Quarantine Quandary

The word quarantine comes from *quaranta giorni*, meaning "40 days" in Venetian, an Italian dialect. During the Black Death in Venice, all ships had to be quarantined for 40 days before going ashore. Today, quarantine is often used under the law, to separate a person who might have been exposed to a disease, from other people. But if infection is confirmed, the patient must be put in isolation, to prevent its spread.

Not a Magic Bullet

Remember Typhoid Mary? She was isolated on an island for the rest of her life! To this day, health officials warn that excessive quarantine is not always a magic bullet (for a quick solution) against a new infectious disease. This decision has to be measured by epidemiology — facts and numbers based on how the disease spreads.

Last But Not Least

In 1855, the third plague pandemic starts from a **rodent** population in Yunnan, China and spreads through rats and humans travelling on the trade routes to the rest of the world. It reaches Hong Kong in 1894, where a French microbiologist finally discovers the culprit. His name is Alexandre Yersin, and the bacterium he finds is named in honour of him.

What's That?

rodent: A group of mammals (including rats) with teeth that keep growing, that need to be gnawed down.

Wow, in French "Rats" are spelt "rats" too!

But in either language they STILL get blamed!

* Aha! The rats are the cause!

茶

Aha! Les rats sont la cause! *

Alexandre Yersin

Despite scientists now suspecting that it was FLEAS which spread it! Hmmph!

We're getting blamed AGAIN?!?

Lockdown in Manchuria

In late 1910, the pneumonic plague lands in Harbin, in northeastern China. It starts from fur hunters, infected by the diseased rodents they hunt. However, in the bitter winter, as people huddle together, the disease spreads rapidly from human to human, killing 60,000. This epidemic is significant because of Wu Lien Teh, a Malaysian-Chinese doctor:

- He invents the use of gauze and cotton masks to prevent infection.
- He **locks down** the city.
- On the first day of the Chinese New Year, even though it is considered bad luck, he cremates thousands of bodies to prevent the spread of the plague.

Did You Know?
Wu Lien Teh used modern methods of epidemiology and science to contain the plague in just four months. The plague is still around today, but can now be treated with antibiotics.

Did You Know?
Quarantine, isolation and **lockdown** are the three tools against infectious disease. A lockdown closes down a city or area from any movement in or out, whether or not the residents are ill.

Wu Lien Teh

HARBIN LOCKDOWN

Use gauze and cotton masks

No one leaves the city

Cremate the dead — even during Chinese New Year

Oh great, blame us rats again... I can't believe that the Chinese term for the Black Death is "鼠疫"... which means "rat plague"...

In Chinese, the word "鼠" (shǔ) means BOTH "rat" and "mouse".

How did we get involved in all this?

THE NOT SO ~~A~~ SPANISH FLU

The 1918–1919 Spanish Flu is so-named not because it happened there, but because Spain is not involved in World War I. As such, Spain is able to freely report the high number of deaths from the flu. Other countries at war suppress this information, not wanting to appear weak. The pandemic kills an estimated 50 million.

Double Whammy

World War I is a perfect setting for the flu to spread. Soldiers are packed closely together where they live, in dirty conditions. Many of them are weak from their wounds, or the stress. The first flu cases are reported in the US, and it is believed that American soldiers, headed to Europe to fight the war, bring the virus with them.

24 June 1918

Dearest mother,
STAND BACK from the PAGE!
and disinfect yourself!
Quite 1/3 of the Battalion and
about 30 of the officers are smitten
with the Spanish Flu.
The hospital overflowed on Friday.
The boys are dropping on parade
like flies in number."

Would I prefer to die in the battlefield or from the flu?

Neither actually...

Did You Know?

Britain's most famous war poet-soldier Wilfred Owen writes to his mum. Owen is killed in action in November that year.

Deadly Defences

For most types of flu, those aged below 5 and above 75 are more at risk. However the Spanish Flu is unusual because it kills more young adults between their 20s and 40s. There are a few possible reasons for this:

- The young adults in this age group have not been exposed to earlier versions of this virus before, and so are harder hit.
- Many catch secondary bacterial infections in their lungs and antibiotics have not been discovered yet.
- A cytokine storm (see page 53).

The Virus Hunters

The search for the Spanish Flu killer virus was a long and protracted one, because it happened before the science was ready.

Frozen Samples

In 1951, 25-year-old Swedish microbiology student Johan Hultin sets out to the **Inuit** village of Brevig Mission (in Alaska), which lost 72 of its 80 inhabitants in five days in November 1918. The burial site has been preserved in **permafrost**. With permission, Hultin collects lung tissue from the bodies. He makes stops on the flight back to desperately try to re-freeze the samples with 'dry ice', or carbon dioxide, from a fire extinguisher. The expedition fails.

A Lifetime's Journey

In 1997 (46 years later), another young microbiologist Jeffery Taubenberger manages to extract parts of the virus RNA from a lung sample preserved from a soldier who died in September 1918. Now 72, Hultin contacts Taubenberger and asks if he would like a frozen sample from Brevig Mission. This time, seven feet down in permafrost, Hultin finds "Lucy", a woman who was in her 20s, with a perfectly preserved lung. By now, there is also a liquid to store and transport the sample to Taubenberger's lab.

Jurassic Park

Much like the Michael Crichton book and movie about dinosaurs recreated from DNA preserved in fossils, scientists in 2005 finally manage to do the same with the Spanish Flu. With "Lucy" and another two samples, they recreate the genome sequence into a viable, live virus.

Did You Know?
This confirms that the Spanish Flu virus is an Influenza A strain of the H1N1 subtype. It is believed to have started as a bird flu strain.

For the LAST TIME I'm the OTHER LUCY OK?

Lucy the Australopithecus (3.2 million years old)

The Influence of Influenza

The flu or influenza is a highly contagious viral infection that affects the respiratory system, causing fever, coughing, a runny nose and severe **malaise**. The virus itself is not identified until the early 1930s. Before that, influenza was an Italian term loosely used for this sickness believed to be caused by the influence of cold wind, and the stars and planets.

What's That?
malaise (mer-leiz): Feeling unwell.

44

A Moving Target

The influenza virus RNA is constantly mutating, which is why it is difficult for a person to develop **immunity** against it. Some new flu strains are similar to old ones, so some people are able to fight it. Other new flu strains are completely different, and these are the ones more likely to cause a pandemic, rather than an epidemic.

Did You Know?

This is why the flu vaccine loses its effectiveness every year, and a new one needs to be developed again. The flu season happens during the winter months and affects a few million people every year.

What's That?

immunity: A body develops an ability to fight a disease when it recognises the virus or bacteria from a previous infection, or vaccination.

2009 H1N1 Flu Pandemic

In 2009, the swine (pig) flu version of H1N1 rears its head in the US and spreads throughout the world. Again, it affects more children and young adults because older people above 60 have seen a similar version of this strain before. This turns out to be a relatively mild pandemic, but still killing 200,000 worldwide.

Did You Know?

Since 1918, there have been two more Influenza A pandemics, in 1957 and 1968, each claiming about one million lives.

Zoonosis Frenzy

All the modern pandemics in the 20th and 21st centuries have been caused by zoonotic, or animal, diseases that have crossed over to humans.

AIDS (Acquired Immunodeficiency Syndrome)

There are two known HIV (Human Immunodeficiency Virus) strains that cause AIDS. They are believed to have passed to humans from wild apes in West and Central Africa. The virus kills cells in the body's immune system, interfering with its ability to fight infection and disease. If not treated quickly to delay the process, HIV develops into AIDS in 8–10 years when the immune system becomes severely damaged, and could lead to death. HIV is only transmitted through contact with bodily fluids or infected needles. HIV/AIDS has been labelled one of the most destructive pandemics in history. About 38 million people are infected with it, and another 32 million have died.

> **Did You Know?**
> It is believed that the virus passed through bush meat, which is meat from wild animals, often eaten in parts of Africa where food is scarce.

You still think I make good eating?

NO TAIL

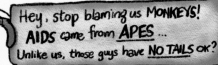

Hey, stop blaming us MONKEYS! AIDS came from APES ... Unlike us, those guys have NO TAILS ok?

TB (Tuberculosis)

A much older disease that has been found in Egyptian mummies thousands of years ago is TB. In 1882, the bacterium, *Mycobacterium tuberculosis* was identified as the bacteria causing it. At that time, the TB pandemic killed one out of every seven people in the US and Europe.

Did You Know?
TB is now the leading killer of people with HIV/AIDS, as they have a weakened immune system.

" ...thus spoke my master, ziggydubsthep... as he wheezed his last ... "Cursed be he who covers not his mouth when coughing and sneezing" "

Mummified cat!

Ebola

Although present in Africa before, the 2013 Ebola Virus Disease outbreak leads to the first epidemic which triggers an international "public health emergency" from the WHO. It is traced to a dead 18-month-old boy in Guinea, in western Africa. Ebola causes fever, body aches and internal bleeding, killing 40% of those who fall ill with it. By 2016, there are more than 11,000 deaths in Guinea, Liberia and Sierra Leone.

Did You Know?
The Ebola virus is believed to reside in bats. In this case, the young child was seen playing near an area infested by bats before he fell sick. His family also confirmed that they ate bat meat.

Apparently.

WE are deadlier than YOU?

47

CORONAVIRUS CONUNDRUM

Corona means "crown" in Latin, and the coronavirus (CoV) is so-named because of the crown-like spikes on its surface. The first deadly epidemic of the 21st century, SARS, is caused by a coronavirus. They are believed to be zoonotic, mutating from animal coronaviruses into stronger killers. However, science has shown that what is strong, also makes it weak.

What's That?
conundrum: A problem that confuses.

Just the Common Cold

The first coronavirus is discovered through an electron microscope in 1937, a strain responsible for an infection in birds, causing deaths in a poultry farm. Later in the 1960s, human coronaviruses are found in the noses of people down with the common cold. There are four such human "common cold" coronaviruses to date.

Antibodies, What Antibodies?

When a virus attacks, antibodies kick in to fight back. This is the basis of immunity. Antibodies are supposed to recognise the virus the next time it appears and defend the body. The science so far suggests that coronavirus antibodies don't last very long, meaning it is possible to be infected again.

Study the Spikes!

"Spike studies" have been happening since SARS. The coronavirus invades a host cell usually in the lung, by latching on with its spikes. Scientists race to develop a vaccine that will teach the body to recognise these spikes and fight back. It usually takes at least 18 months from idea to an actual vaccine.

SARS-CoV

The SARS coronavirus, named SARS-CoV, killed 10% of infected patients. It is found to be almost identical to a coronavirus in bats, which is believed to have first jumped across species to the civet cat, then to humans. In 2003, these civet cats were sold live for meat, or pets, in markets in Guangdong, China, where SARS started.

MERS-CoV

The MERS (Middle East Respiratory Syndrome) coronavirus has a 35% fatality rate and is believed to have also started as a bat virus, but passed through camels before infecting humans. The MERS epidemic in the Middle East in 2012 was mostly contained within that region, and tended to spread only in hospitals at very close contact with the infected. In 2015, an infected person travelled to South Korea, causing an outbreak there.

What Makes It Stronger Makes It Weak

Both SARS and MERS were eventually contained,
and did not spread much further to become pandemics.
Their deadly character, was to be their own undoing.

When the virus is too deadly, the host (the patient) dies before it spreads, killing the virus itself, which can't survive without a host.

Conversely, over time, the virus tends to mutate to a milder version to ensure its own survival in its hosts.

SARS and MERS work deep inside people's lungs, making them more deadly, but also less likely to spread, compared to a virus that operates further up at the nose and throat.

What's That?

R_0 or R-nought, measures the number of cases an infected person will generate.

If the virus has a strong need to spread, the ability to cut off this spread is equally strong. When every infected person is isolated, the reproduction number, or R_0, of the virus drops rapidly.

A Too Strong Defence = Death

The SARS and MERS coronaviruses both target cells in a patient's lungs, causing death when the lungs fail. However, the mechanism that kills at the end is sometimes due to the body mounting too strong a defence, and attacking itself.

This is the coronavirus' **modus operandi**:

Loads of copies: The virus enters through the throat or nose, taking over healthy host cells and making copies of itself. When the viral load is heavy enough, it enters the lungs.

The body strikes back: Alerted to the presence of this viral invader, the body's defences fight back, calling immune cells into the lungs. The patient runs a fever from the inflammation in the lungs and experiences shortness of breath. At this stage, the body could beat the virus for good (or not).

> **What's That?**
>
> **modus operandi**:
> Sometimes shortened as M.O. In this case, it refers to the way the coronavirus operates.

A Storm in the Lungs

In some cases, the body's own immune system overreacts. It sends an army of immune cells which floods the lungs, killing everything in the way. This is called a **cytokine storm** — when immune cell proteins accumulate too much, blocking the airways and causing death.

Did You Know?
When scientists study the lungs of those who have died, they find thickened and scarred lung tissue as a result of this deadly battle in the lungs.

Out of Body Breathing

For patients in this critical stage of lung infection (pneumonia), some need extra support to breathe while their lungs repair. This could be through:

Mechanical ventilation: A breathing mask or tube artificially helps a patient to exchange gases the way breathing functions.

ECMO (Extracorporeal Membrane Oxygenation): Literally, the patient's blood is oxygenated outside the body, carbon dioxide removed, and put back in, like a lung **bypass**.

> ### What's That?
> **bypass**: ECMO is more commonly known for its use during a heart bypass, where the machine runs the heart's functions while the heart is being operated on.

Coping with Intensive Care

Such life-saving equipment is only possible in a hospital's Intensive Care Unit (ICU), with specialist doctors and nurses in full protective gear. In a pandemic, if infection cases rise too fast and a high volume of patients need lung support, not all healthcare systems would be able to cope.

The Younger Are 'Stronger'

There have been no deaths in children from SARS and MERS and those who get infected show mild or no symptoms. This could also mean that not all cases in children are reported, resulting in low infection numbers in this age group.

Children are said to have better natural immunity than adults. This is the most basic and least complicated defence in humans which gets to work right away when viruses and other germs invade.

Sometimes simple is better...

No storms... Just a shower...

The immune system of a child is still developing and not fully mature. It doesn't fight back so robustly as to cause a cytokine storm.

Scientists have only been able to confirm epidemiology numbers that show children are spared from these coronaviruses, but have not yet discovered why exactly this is so.

COVID-19

On the very last day of 2019, a mysterious pneumonia is reported to the WHO, immediately rousing past memories of the terror that was SARS. The report comes from Wuhan, an 11-million population port city in Hubei province in China. In early January, the first patient dies: the first of thousands of deaths in Hubei in those months.

Did You Know?
Within a week, the virus responsible is identified as a novel (new) coronavirus.

The Perfect Storm

It is the year 2020. Various factors contribute to an explosion of infections by this new coronavirus.

- The **epicentre**, Wuhan, is deep in winter. Residents are mostly indoors, in cold, dry and enclosed spaces.

- 春运 (chūn yùn) or spring migration, the largest human migration on earth every year, has started in earnest. The Chinese are heading home in the two weeks before the New Year celebrations on 25 January 2020.

- Add to this potent mix — travel around the globe is at the highest level ever since the last pandemic. Humans are the perfect hosts to carry infection round the world.

What's That?

epicentre: The centre of an earthquake, also used to mean the centre of a crisis.

Did You Know?

January is barely up when the WHO declares the Wuhan outbreak a Public Health Emergency of International Concern.

武汉封城

Two days before the Chinese New Year, the government locks down the tens of millions of people in Wuhan, the rest of Hubei province and some affected cities. All transport networks are shut down and road blocks are put up to stop people from entering or leaving. A "people's war" is declared against this new virus.

> ## Did You Know?
> 武汉封城
> (wǔ hàn fēng chéng): literally, the sealing of the city of Wuhan.

Desperate Times Call for Desperate Measures

This drastic move makes a tremendous impact on the Chinese and the world. Faced with a mysterious killer virus and cut off from the rest of the world, to some, it feels like an apocalypse, or the end of days. For the next seven weeks, the world watches in horror as the daily tally for infected patients, and deaths, keep going up.

> ## Did You Know?
> Unfortunately, this is a scene that plays out in other countries in the following months, as infection numbers rise rapidly in countries like Italy, Iran, the UK and US.

Same Same but Different

The International Committee on **Taxonomy** of Viruses is responsible for naming the new virus, **SARS-CoV-2**. It is genetically very similar to the SARS coronavirus, and also believed to have originated from bats. Viruses are named this way to help scientists develop test kits, vaccines and medicines.

The WHO names diseases more generally, under the International Classification of Diseases (ICD), to enable discussion on prevention and spread. On 11 February 2020, the disease caused by SARS-CoV-2 is named the Coronavirus Disease 2019, or **COVID-19**.

Too Little, Too Late?

In mid-March, China's daily infection numbers finally taper off to much lower numbers — early indication that this largest quarantine in history has worked. Depending on whose perspective, China's bold approach has slowed the course of a rapidly spreading and deadly disease. Yet, some ask if this is too little, too late because on 11 March 2020, the WHO declares COVID-19 a pandemic.

Once Bitten Twice Shy

Singapore, a travel hub and tourist destination, is one of the first countries the COVID-19 reaches. On the same day of the China lockdown, a 66-year-old tourist from Wuhan is tested positive for the virus. The country immediately swings into action, having put processes and systems in place since SARS 17 years ago. The Singapore M.O.:

- Temperature screening, and questions asked of every traveller based on their travel history.

- As numbers rise, it puts all returning Singaporeans on a mandatory 14-day "Stay Home Notice". Short term visitors are not allowed in at all.

- Quickly developing **test kits** based on information shared by scientists working on the SARS-CoV-2 genome sequence all over the world.

- The just-opened **National Centre for Infectious Diseases (NCID)** is built precisely to cope much better, the next time a killer virus like SARS appears. It has 330 beds, full isolation rooms and lung support equipment.

> **Did You Know?**
> The **NCID** is a self-contained facility which can be locked down if needed. Its capacity can also be increased to 500 beds during an outbreak.

EXPERIENCE FROM 2003

The Science Detectives

The pressing need is for a test kit to confirm infection in patients. From day one, scientists work intensively to churn out various kits to do the job quickly and accurately. In another month, there is a swab test used at all checkpoints on visitors coming into Singapore.

The Life Cycle of a Swab Test

A long, sterile, fibre-tipped stick is inserted into the nose and a 'swab' taken. This swab sample is taken from hospitals, or from Singapore's land, sea and air checkpoints to a lab. The RNA is extracted from the swab and converted into a more stable DNA. It is then put through a polymerase chain reaction (PCR), a common tool in microbiology. This amplifies the signal from the virus so it can be detected.

> **Did You Know?**
> The eventual aim is always to develop a **test kit** that can show results on the spot, without having to send it to a lab for processing.

Connecting the Dots

As the number of cases are reported every day, identifying the source in clusters of infection is the top priority.

19 January: Two infected Wuhan tourists visit church A, starting a cluster there.

7 February: The first infection is reported in a man who was also there that same day. Singapore's first death, six weeks later, is also from this cluster.

12 February: The first infection at church B. The man had no travel history to China. Over the next week, more cases emerge at this church.

At this point, contact tracers work hard to track the source of infection, because until it is found, this mystery source could keep the infection cycle going.

A Detective's Instinct

The Criminal Investigation Department, or the CID, is the perfect candidate for this new puzzle. The detectives sieve through large amounts of information from interviews and camera footage exactly the same way they would solve a crime. The eureka moment comes when they find out that:

What's That?

eureka moment: The "aha!" moment when something is solved.

25 January: A man from church B had in fact attended the same Chinese New Year party as a couple from church A! There was, however, a big BUT — this couple was not infected with COVID-19.

CRIMINAL INVESTIGATION DEPARTMENT

MOST WANTED!

COVID-19 VIRUS

Missing Link Found

Scientists quickly develop a blood test to detect the presence of COVID-19 antibodies, which proves the couple had in fact been recently infected. Both had been unwell and had sought treatment, but were not tested for COVID-19 earlier.

Flatten The Curve

What's That?
flatten the curve: This means to lower the rate of infections.

Initially the worst-hit country with the highest number of infections after China, Singapore falls much further behind as many countries start to report infection numbers. The strategy is to identify, report and isolate cases with the aim to **flatten the curve** on the rise of infections. This would enable the healthcare system to cope with infected patients, and not be overwhelmed.

INFECTIONS

Circuit Breakers

On a day-to-day basis, "social" or "safe distancing" becomes a new buzzword. Since the virus is spread by contact, especially over shared meals and socialising, the only way is to apply **circuit breakers** to the process. In many affected countries, large gatherings and events are cancelled, schools are closed, and people work from home.

Quick Change Artist

The behaviour of this virus is much harder to pin down. It proves to spread more easily than other deadly coronaviruses and is hard to track, leaving "distancing" as the most effective way to stop it.

- It presents both in the lungs, as well as in the upper respiratory tract (nose and throat).
- It infects young and old patients.
- Some do not show symptoms nor have a fever, but are still infectious.

The Math of Infections

As infections keep rising, mathematicians crunch the global COVID-19 numbers which are increasing exponentially. This means a number starts small, but keeps doubling over time on a steep climb up a graph. Without circuit breakers, these are the perfect conditions for unlimited spread:

1. There is at least one infected person in the population.

2. There is regular contact between the infected and the uninfected.

3. There are large numbers of uninfected hosts with the potential to be infected.

This math confirms the science that if
(a) the infected isolate
(b) most people stay home
(c) and as early as possible
the rate of infection will drop dramatically, and the curve on the graph will flatten.

Did You Know?

A significant number of COVID-19 patients lose their sense of taste and smell. Scientists say the numbers are enough for this to be used as a first symptom to self-isolate, before confirming infection (or not).

A Tale of Two Countries

Singapore, South Korea, Hong Kong and Taiwan have had their 'dress rehearsal' through SARS, MERS and the 2009 H1N1 flu. But not all countries are able to cope as they have.

South Korea: Initially facing a steep curve with infected numbers hitting 8,000 in the first few weeks, South Korea's daily numbers also drop. This is thanks to testing thousands for infection every day, up-to-date phone alerts, quarantine under the law, and a population committed to good hygiene and shutting down contact.

Italy: On 30 January 2020, Italy sees its first COVID-19 cases. However, by late March, it outstrips Singapore and South Korea and becomes the second country with the largest number of cases after China. On some days, it has 900 deaths, partly due to a large number of elderly. Unable to go with an identify-and-isolate model, Italy locks down the whole country.

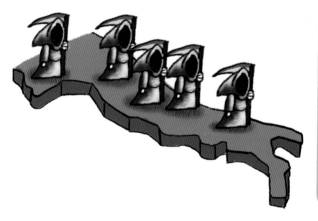

Did You Know?

In early March 2020, the epicentre of the epidemic moves to Europe. By late March, the US streaks to the top of the table with the highest number of cases.

World War III

In some countries, fighting COVID-19 becomes an all-too-real war. Most patients (80%) experience mild symptoms, but 15% have lung infection and might need ventilators to help with breathing. Another 5% fall critically ill when their lungs or other organs fail, leading to some deaths.

Wartime Triage

In war, triage involves deciding who to treat first among many injured soldiers, based on who is more likely to recover. In countries like Spain and Italy, doctors have to choose which patient to put on ventilators because there simply aren't enough. Many have to make the painful decision to save younger patients with more 'life-years' and let go of older ones who are likely to die.

Field Hospitals

Like a scene out of the world wars, some countries — Italy, Spain, France, the UK and US — set up field hospitals to cope with numbers.

Domino Theory

COVID-19 spreads to almost every country and territory in the world. Eventually, most countries close their borders and air travel shuts down. At home, many countries opt for various versions of lockdown to keep people away from each other. In the US, some states put in a **"shelter-in-place"** order — which is to enforce staying home under the law.

A Chain Is as Strong as the Weakest Link

In 2020, countries hunker down for the long haul with the COVID-19 contagion. Even as countries like China and Singapore contain it early, a fresh wave of infections hit them as their citizens overseas return. Governments, health officials, doctors, scientists and people on the street — what they do (or do not do) will game change the direction of this virus.

Did You Know?

Shelter-in-place is a war term used to refer to situations where it is not safe to step outside.
Domino theory is a Cold War term used to refer to the belief that events in one country could cause neighbouring countries to 'topple' the same way.

HAVE VIRUS WILL TRAVEL

Pandemics in the 21st century have one thing their predecessors didn't have — the ability to fly, cruise and be transported to almost any spot in the world. This has become a pandemic's best partner in crime.

No Royal Treatment

In late January, a man leaves the cruise ship, Diamond Princess, when it docks in Hong Kong. As the ship almost reaches its next destination, Yokohama in Japan, it receives news that this man has tested positive for the new coronavirus. Japan decides against letting the passengers, who might have been infected, ashore.

DIAMOND PRINCESS

A Comedy of Errors

The ship is put on a 14-day quarantine. At the end of it, there are more than 700 infections, and a reported eight deaths, providing an early lesson for the world, to never underestimate an invisible enemy.

- Those who had contact with the first infected man were not removed, but told to stay in their rooms. They continued to move about the ship and eat from the buffets.

- When the first 10 passengers tested positive, they were evacuated, but the remaining 3,000+ people were kept on board with no proper infection control in place.

- The ship was registered in the UK, but was on Japanese territory. It was not clear where the responsibility for the ship lay. It largely fell on the hands of the crew, who were ill-equipped with skills to cope with an infectious disease.

Floating Petri Dishes

Scientists describe these cruise ships as 'floating' Petri dishes, in this case it hastened the spread of the virus within a closed environment. The ship should not have been used for quarantine, where the infected and non-infected mixed freely.

Why do I feel like I'm in a LAB?

SS PETRI

Cruise to Nowhere

An estimated 20 ships, with thousands of passengers on board, are left out at sea at the height of the global COVID-19 crisis. Most of them are not able to get permission to dock and those who manage to, are left quarantined off the shore.

Hey, watch it!

Move a bit, will you?

Don't crowd!

STOP PUSHING!

You're too close!

Move aside!

Oops

Swaps at Sea

A ship-to-ship rescue occurs off the coast of Panama in late March. A cruise company uses one of its ships to send staff, supplies and COVID-19 test kits to its stranded liner. Another two ships near Phuket, Thailand do 'passenger swaps' and then go on separate journeys to send passengers home to the UK, and Australia and New Zealand.

Grounded

International air travel comes to a grinding halt, as countries restrict or ban tourists from coming in and discourage citizens from travelling out. Most global flights are suspended and the future of airline companies is up in the air, losing hundreds of billions of dollars.

Did You Know?

A few hundred Singapore Airlines cabin crew retrain, to become "care ambassadors" in hospitals.

All Surfaces Are Not Created Equal

Scientists discover that the coronavirus resides within a fatty layer that allows it to survive outside its host. They use a **nebuliser** to mimic an infected person coughing out the virus into the air, then they test how long the virus survives on surfaces.

What's That?
nebuliser: A medical device used to produce a fine spray of liquid.

- In the air — 3 hours
- Copper — 4 hours
- Cardboard — 24 hours
- Plastic and stainless steel — 2–3 days

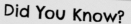

SOAP MOLECULES

Did You Know?
Soap molecules attach themselves to the fatty layer on the coronavirus, and destroy it, and everything then washes away with water.

A CRISIS OF FEAR

In every pandemic in the past, the 'virus' of fear has always spread faster than the virus itself. Fighting a rising sense of panic and **irrational** fear is all part of battling this war.

What's That?
irrational: Not rational, without reason or logic.

An Information Pandemic

Until the mid 2000s, news was still fed to consumers mostly through newspapers and on TV. In the last decade, social media has exploded into a massive lifestyle tool. This means that from the get-go, there has been a blow-by-blow account of every infection, every death and all manner of real and fake news.

Did You Know?
This has made instant information a double-edged sword — providing relevant and helpful information to fight the COVID-19 virus, but also spreading fear, rumours and **stigma**.

What's That?
stigma: A set of negative or unfair beliefs about a group of people.

Axe the Xenophobia

In the face of disease and fear, some people lose their moral compass. They target Chinese and people of Asian descent around the world. This happens on a few levels:

- Hate speech, calling COVID-19 a 'Chinese' or 'yellow' virus. One newspaper headline refers to the "Chinese virus pandamonium" (a pun on pandemonium, which means disorder or confusion, and a reference to the Chinese panda).

- Mild aggression, where Chinese or Asians are not allowed into shops or restaurants, or evicted by their landlords.

- Hate crime, where Chinese or Asians are spat on, beaten up and told to "get out".

> **Did You Know?**
>
> In some cases, healthcare workers in uniform are also shunned on public transport, for fear they might be carrying the virus. This invites even greater condemnation, for these are the heroes on the front-line.

> **What's That?**
> xenophobia: Dislike of or prejudice against people from other countries.

Everybody Loves a Clean Bottom

In many cities, as COVID-19 takes root, a strange **phenomenon** occurs. People panic-buy essentials like rice, pasta and canned food, but also clear out the shelves of toilet paper. Social media posts show empty toilet paper aisles and videos of people brawling over toilet paper. Fortunately, it also gives birth to witty lines and memes for humankind to have a good laugh at themselves!

Did You Know?

In Australia, a newspaper went so far as to print eight extra pages in a special "emergency toilet paper" edition, should people, ahem, run out of rolls.

What's That?

phenomenon: An extraordinary occurrence.

Science of Stockpiling

There are a few theories offered:

- Toilet rolls are large and take up a lot of shelf space. When these shelves are cleared out, it creates a greater impact on the mind that something has run out.

- This fear of missing out (FOMO) spreads, especially with photos and videos posted on social media, giving the impression that toilet paper supply is drying up.

- Some say this is clearly a **First World problem**, meaning the concern is no longer about getting enough food, but the comforts of using a toilet.

$Caremongers and the Contagion of Kindness

With rising deaths, and distancing measures in place, movements sprout around the world to spread care instead. In Canada, where the term "caremongering" started, social media groups open up within communities to help the elderly with groceries and errands. These #viralkindness campaigns spread everywhere.

Companies in Combat

Companies, big and small, switch gears to change their core business to support this battle.

- Apple, Tesla, Mercedes and global car makers adapt their factories to make ventilators or their parts.

- HP starts a global outreach for their partners to 3D-print face shields and parts for a portable ventilator so that more can be quickly produced.

- With most of the world's children (estimated 1.5 billion) staying home, Lego engages children with a daily #letsbuildtogether challenge.

Let There be Cake!

In crisis, humanity has also shown an amazing ability to live, laugh and love. In Italy, a bar serves "aperitiviruses" (as opposed to an **apéritif**) and elsewhere, "Corona cake" is served, fashioned as a spiky cream ball.

As Easter approaches, and egg hunts are cancelled, a French chocolatier, fed up with so much news on the virus, produces a spiky COVID-19 Easter egg.

What's That?
apéritif: A drink served before a meal to whet the appetite.

THE POWER OF QUESTIONS

The year 2020 sees the unprecedented use of the word "**unprecedented**".

- For a virus that infects and kills in numbers that keep climbing.

- For a lockdown in many parts of the world.

- For new social norms that tell people to distance themselves.

- For an information flow that has become **torrential**.

What's That?
unprecedented: Never done or known before.

torrential: Falling in a forceful way.

The Tale of My Classmate's Uncle

The BBC (British Broadcasting Corporation) investigates a viral post going round the world that is estimated to have reached millions.

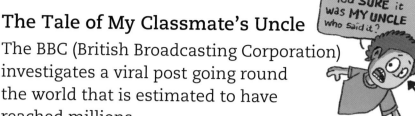

> My classmate's uncle and nephew, graduated with a master's degree, and works in Shenzhen Hospital. He is being transferred to study Wuhan pneumonia virus. He just called me and told me to tell my friends…
>
> **Read more**
>
> 5:28 AM

It starts in early February and hops across social media as posts and personal messages.

- It tells people to wash their hands, which is good advice.
- It also tells people the new coronavirus presents as a dry cough only and not in a runny nose, which is not always true.
- It says the virus "hates the sun", which is also not proven.
- It advises a coronavirus "self-check", to hold your breath for more than 10 seconds to "prove" you are virus-free.

Along the way, the viral post mutates, attributing the expert named in the message to Japanese, Taiwanese or Stanford doctors. The post gets translated and goes viral further in several languages.

Did You Know?

This post goes viral by copypasta, **urban lingo** for when a post is copied and pasted, and not shared from the original post. This gives the impression that it really originated from somebody's "classmate's uncle".

What's That?

urban lingo: 'Urban' language or slang that develops in popular culture, not usually in a dictionary.

Fact Checkers

An independent fact-checking charity called Full Fact in the UK and American fact-checking site, Snopes, pursue the truth behind this post. They counter it line by line, with medical information from the WHO, the US Centres for Disease Control and Prevention (CDC) and the UK National Health Service (NHS).

Dolphins in Venice

The National Geographic also tackles happy but fake animal news circulating on social media. The news is shared by hundreds and thousands of people taken in by news about wildlife bouncing back, in a world with much fewer humans.

Did You Know?

Another post, about swans returning to canals in Venice, was put together by a woman from India who mistakenly used a photo of swans in Burano about 9 km (5.5 mi) away from Venice. Her tweet gets more than a million likes.

FICTION	FACT
As tourists disappear, dolphins have returned to the waters of Venice.	The dolphins were filmed at a port in Sardinia, almost 800 km (500 mi) away.
As humans "social distance", elephants in Yunnan, China come out to play and get drunk on 30 kg (66 lb) of corn wine.	The source of the photo could not be found, but Chinese media confirm this is not true.

Did You Know?

You can try to search the origin of a photo with a programme like TinEye, or do a reverse image search on Google!

According to this article, I was found DRUNK in a field?!

But you don't even drink alcohol!

And I've never even been to Italy!

Will you humans PLEASE leave us animals out of your FAKE NEWS?

The Earth Was Once Flat

Science is a study that constantly **evolves** with society, and now, with the way information spreads. What is taken to be fact or science at one point, can and will evolve to a newer, proven science further on. One example is the belief, millennia ago, that the earth was flat. In pandemics, it's miasma:

- Early scientists in the Middle Ages and also ancient China put forth theories about disease based on patterns they see. (For example, people got sick around rot and foul smells.)

- Two thousand years later, early scientists like Louis Pasteur confirm their belief that microscopic bacteria and viruses are the culprits in disease.

- Only in the 20th century, are scientists able to see and confirm the physical presence of the virus.

- By the 21st century, scientists are able to quickly identify and put together the DNA of a new invisible enemy, and even recreate it in a lab.

The Power of Questions

The quest to find answers in science never changes. Scientists continue to confirm or **debunk** theories through testing and analysing data, to find out how and why. The results are published in journals and online, and reviewed by fellow scientists and doctors (called a peer review). Journalists then crunch this data and present it in the news.

MY ^Pandemic NOTES

Dear Reader,

We've left this section blank for you to write or draw your notes, and make this book yours.

Now that you've read *Invisible Enemies*, what is your plan? What is the disease? How does it behave? And what are the effective weapons against its spread? What can YOU do?

Let's put our battle plan together. We can do this!

Love,

HWEE'S HANDBOOK TOOLKIT

Here's how to put together an accurate report from facts you find in books and online. A report that you publish could be for school, or something you share on social media, or just something you tell your friends.

YAK YADDA YAK YADDA YAK

YAK YAK

?? CAN YOU SIMPLIFY THAT?

MY STORY
What Is the Angle?

What is the question you want answered or the point you want to make? Narrow this down to one or two sentences. For example, the angle of this book is "to arm every reader with knowledge on pandemics, to empower him or her to act against these invisible enemies."

Who Is the Audience?

Is it a general audience or your parents or friends? Put yourself in the shoes of your audience and write or speak in a way that will connect with them.

Do you know what he's saying?

No idea ? Sorry, I don't speak cat

MY RESEARCH
Too Good to Be True

It usually is, but sometimes, fact is stranger than fiction. The more you read, the sharper your 'sensor' will be on whether something is real or fake.

Cross-check!

If a strange fact or piece of news is true, other news outlets are likely to have it too. Check other credible sources to back up your information. If you're ready, you can also read up on science journals and other investigative reports.

Numbers

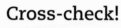

In reports on the same topic, numbers and other finer details might differ, depending on the research methods of the writer. Based on the many reports, you could give an estimated number. (You can see how it's been done in this book.)

Red Flags

Does this piece of information stir up negative emotions? Does it over-generalise the information? For example, a statement like "Any solution with 70% alcohol kills the coronavirus" is based on results discovered in a lab. But "Drinking hot whisky cures a man's coronavirus", probably isn't.

It's TERRIBLE!

It's HORRIBLE!

Oh no... what happened?

His favourite TV SHOW just got cancelled...

MY REPORT
Pause and Parse

Language itself, could also be used to connect or persuade more powerfully. For example, something **bad** could be **terrible**, **horrifying** or **devastating**. After reading up, decide for yourself which it is.

What's That?
parse: To break up and analyse a sentence.

WHO TOLD YOU THIS?

A little bird...

OH YEAH? WHICH "little bird"?

Who Says?

You must always be clear who the source of your information is before you publish. Is this a person, or organisation you trust with a track record of accuracy? If you're not clear, hold the information until you are, or discard it.

You? No

Your Opinion

What do you think? After observing patterns and behaviours in what you have read, form your opinion based on facts. This will add value to what you publish.

WHO? WHAT? WHEN? HOW?

Check and Check. Then Check Again. And Again.

How? WHO? WHAT?

WHY? Before you publish or share, check your facts and your writing. Then check again! When working on this book, I spent as much time checking the material over and again, as researching and writing it.

HOW? WHO?

WHEN? WHAT? WHY? HOW? WHY?

WHAT? WHO?

KNOWLEDGE IS POWER

This phrase is commonly credited to English philosopher, Francis Bacon, on the pursuit of science. There have been many versions of this saying in the history of mankind. 用智铺谋 (yòng zhì pù móu) is to use knowledge (and wisdom) to put together a battle plan, especially when an enemy is invisible.

In the battle against a foe unseen... your best sword lies within...

No, but for a HUMAN, he makes a lot of sense...

Francis Bacon... related to us?

Wow, great quotation!

Wait, are you sure he said that?

Yeah, how do you know it's by HIM?

EDITOR'S NOTE:
WELL-SPOTTED READER!
THAT QUOTATION ISN'T BY FRANCIS BACON.
IT WAS MADE UP BY OUR ARTIST *BASED* ON BACON'S IDEA!

ACKNOWLEDGEMENTS

Lots of Thank Yous to:

Agency for Science, Technology and Research (Singapore);

Ministry of Communications and Information (Singapore);

Institute of Policy Studies (Singapore);

Lydia and Mindy, my amazing people from
Marshall Cavendish International (Asia);

Chua Mui Hoong, Soon Minh, Alex Yue and my greatest
counsel, Dr Yue Wai Mun. He makes sure that I do not try
to be the scientist in this endeavour. Instead, to quote
his constant refrain, "the truth at any one point is only
true at that time, and should be subject to every child's
own inquiry."

ABOUT
HWEE AND DAVID

Trained at the Northwestern University Medill School of Journalism, former CNA (Channel NewsAsia) reporter and editor **Hwee Goh** put together this handbook from books and a few hundred sources online. She is grateful to the scientists, doctors, epidemiologists and researchers for their meticulous work in published  journals, as well as her journalism colleagues all over the world. Hwee is now a media and editorial consultant. She continues to curate stories on @hweezbooks.

 Illustrator **David Liew** and Hwee were in junior college together studying strange but true moments in 15th and 16th century Europe. David continued on to be a history teacher before becoming illustrator to many bestselling book series. David's art often takes on humorous angles appreciated by his fans, young and old. It is with this added layer of art, that the Change Makers team hopes to engage young readers on their own journey of discovery into this world's unknowns.